George, the Best of All!

Ingrid Lee

with illustrations by
Stéphane Denis

ORCA BOOK PUBLISHERS

Library and Archives Canada Cataloguing in Publication

Lee, Ingrid, 1948-
George, the best of all / Ingrid Lee;
with illustrations by Stéphane Denis.
(Orca echoes)

Sequel to: George most wanted.

ISBN 1-55143-623-X

I. Denis, Stéphane, 1971- II. Title. III. Series.

PS8623.E44G45 2006   jC813'.6   C2006-903013-8

First published in the United States: 2006
Library of Congress Control Number: 2006927082

Summary: George, the little red plastic guy, is back, more famous than ever!

Orca Book Publishers gratefully acknowledges the support for its publishing programs
provided by the following agencies: the Government of Canada through the Book Publishing
Industry Development Program and the Canada Council for the Arts, and the Province of
British Columbia through the BC Arts Council and the Book Publishing Tax Credit.

Design and typesetting by Doug McCaffry

Cover and interior illustrations by Stéphane Denis

Orca Book Publishers   Orca Book Publishers
PO Box 5626 Station B   PO Box 468
Victoria, BC Canada   Custer, WA USA
V8R 6S4   98240-0468

www.orcabook.com
Printed and bound in Canada
Printed on recycled paper, 60% PCW.
09 08 07 06 • 4 3 2 1

Before the Story Begins

George was a little guy made out of plastic. He had pink skin and black hair. He always wore a red jumpsuit and shiny red shoes.

On fireworks day, Katie and Mackenzie tied George to a dragon rocket. George's parts flew apart. Only one leg and shoe landed back in Katie and Mackenzie's yard.

The children tried to find the rest of George. They made "Most Wanted" posters. The Scarborough Windows newspaper wrote a story about the missing parts.

The posters and the newspaper story worked. They worked too well! Too many strange plastic parts ended up at Katie and Mackenzie's house.

Katie and Mackenzie put the extra pieces together. They made some new plastic figures. George ended up a little bit different.

During the adventure, George found an amazing machine. He took it for a ride and disappeared.

Katie and Mackenzie shook their heads.

What's that little guy up to now?

Reporter Dan
Writes a Story

A three-wheeled bike zoomed out of Katie and Mackenzie's driveway. The rider leaned into the wind. He was a little plastic guy with a red jumpsuit and shiny red shoes. You couldn't see his big blue eyes. He wore goggles. You couldn't see his wavy black hair. A helmet covered the top of his head.

Rrrrrr...rum rum rrrrum!

The bike roared louder than a barking dog, louder than a lawn mower.

The grumpy old man next door was trimming his roses. "Dang!" he complained. "Those kids should keep their toys in the house. An old man like me shouldn't have to listen to all that racket."

The little rider kept right on zooming. One pink plastic hand swung into the air.

Mr. Mohan and his boy were sitting on their front porch eating blackberry muffins. They watched the toy sail past their porch. It looked like the rider was waving.

Mr. Mohan and his boy waved back.

Some kids were playing basketball in the schoolyard. The bike raced by the fence. "Hey!" yelled one of the kids. "There goes George."

Another kid nodded. "That's Katie's boyfriend," she said.

All the kids in the schoolyard ran over to the fence. They waved at the plastic figure. Then they went back to shooting baskets.

Reporter Dan stood at the end of the street. He was measuring a pothole in the road.

That hole was a mystery. Maybe lightning struck the road. Maybe a gopher wanted a new home. Maybe no one paid their taxes.

Reporter Dan was writing a story about the pothole for the *Scarborough Windows* newspaper. A photographer was there too. He was taking a picture of the pothole.

The triker hit the pothole and dumped the rider. Just then the camera clicked.

Oh oh!

The photographer looked at the camera display screen. "Hey, Dan!" he exclaimed. "Look at this picture. There's a little plastic guy in the pothole. He's waving at me."

Reporter Dan chewed his pencil. He shook his head. "Some people will do anything to get their picture in the paper," he said.

The reporter and the photographer hurried back to the newspaper office. There was no time to take another picture.

George
Connects the Dots

George shot down the street on his green machine. He leaned back and tilted his face to the sun. He stretched out his hand to catch a breeze.

Bam! The bike smacked into a giant crater.

Pop! The front tire burst. Bits of rubber blasted into the air.

George flipped over the back wheels. His goggles snapped. His helmet bounced away. The bike did a wheelie and raced off all by itself.

George sat up. He was lucky. At least he still had his head!

He was a bit dizzy, though. Stars flashed in his eyes. Lights dotted the sky. They blinked and twinkled and razzled and dazzled. Some of them were red. Some of them were green. Some of them were pink and blue.

George knew how to connect the dots of light. He drew lines in his head from one dot to the next. He drew a pot out of stars—a pot bigger than the pothole! And he drew a horse—an astronomical white horse!

He was George the Brave, George the Steadfast, George the Astronomer. He would ride that horse. He would be a star too!

The Pickup Driver Visits the Carnival

The pickup driver stopped his truck for a red light. It was dark. He saw a pothole in the truck's headlights.

"Hey!" said the pickup driver. "That looks like George. What's that guy doing in the middle of the road?"

The pickup driver got out and picked up the little guy. Then he drove his truck into the mall parking lot.

Johnny's Joy Town was set up at the end of the parking lot. Pink and blue lightbulbs popped on and off. A carnival man was polishing the corn-dog cart.

The pickup driver got out of his truck. "Wow!" he said to the carnie. "This is a pretty fancy carnival. What rides you got?"

"I got a Fun Slide and a Screamer," the carnie said. "And I got a merry-go-round and a Ferris wheel. You can't have a carnival without those two. Those rides are what everybody likes."

The merry-go-round had a white horse with blue stars. It had a silver saddle and leather stirrups.

"That's a mighty fine horse," said the pickup driver.

The carnival man looked at the horse sadly. "It's late. All the kids are gone. You can have a ride for half price."

What the heck! The pickup driver had a loonie in his pocket. He gave the loonie to the carnie and climbed on the white horse with the silver saddle. He put George on the saddle too.

The merry-go-round began to turn. The horses went faster and faster.

"Yahoo!" yelled the pickup driver.

After the ride, the pickup driver looked down the midway. He eyed the Ferris wheel.

The carnie shook his head. "I'm shutting down," he said. "Spy wants her walk."

"That's a funny name," said the pickup driver.

"Spy's my partner," the carnie said. "She's a monkey."

The pickup driver and the carnie waved good-bye. The pink and blue lights went out.

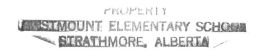
15

George
Rides a White Horse

George swung himself up on the silver saddle. He grabbed the reins. The white horse full of blue stars bolted into the night.

Giddy up! Giddy up!

The wind blew through the dark waves in George's hair. It whistled past his ears.

Giddy up! Giddy up!

George felt the muscles of his mighty mount between his legs. He felt the horsepower. His bronco ran so fast that the horse in front couldn't get away. His bronco ran so fast that the horse behind couldn't catch up.

George stood up in the saddle and waved his hand in the air. He went up and down, up and down. The lights of the night sky glittered in his eyes.

He would get himself a hat. He would get himself a pair of silver spurs to match his silver saddle. He would blaze a new trail clear across the country!

The Carnie and Spy
Go For a Walk

Spy waited for the carnie in their trailer. The monkey was polishing her nails. She had already put on her best bib.

"Hello, m'darling!" boomed the carnie. "It's time for our walk."

The carnie and Spy stayed away from the lights of the mall. They walked under the Ferris wheel. They walked past the Screamer. All the rides were dark and quiet.

Spy sat on the carnie's shoulder. She cleaned out his ear. She twisted his hair. She pulled out a loose thread on his collar. Then she saw George sitting on the silver saddle.

Spy grabbed George in her little paws. She turned him upside down and gave him a shake. She twisted

his head round and round. Maybe the monkey thought George was a saltshaker. Maybe she thought he was a pepper grinder. Who knows what goes on in a monkey's head?

The carnie man leaned against an empty shopping cart. He gave his monkey a kiss. "How about a peanut?" he said.

A peanut! Spy dropped George into the cart and held out her hands.

When the carnie pulled the peanuts out of his pocket, the loonie slipped out. It landed in the shopping cart too. It landed in George's lap.

The man and his monkey munched peanuts and watched the stars.

"Excuse me," said a skinny kid with braces. "This cart has to go back into the mall. The mall is closing."

"Sure, kid," said the carnie. "Want a peanut?"

Spy and the carnival man went back to the trailer. "We need to go shopping one of these days," said the man. "Your bottle of nail polish is just about empty."

Katie and Mackenzie
Play House

Katie sat at the kitchen table. She was drawing on a piece of paper.

Mr. Dab, Battle Ram and the girl sat on the table. Yellow Melon sat on the *Scarborough Windows* newspaper.

Mackenzie walked into the room. He looked at all the plastic people. "What are you doing?" he asked his sister.

"I'm playing house," Katie said. "Yellow Melon makes the money. She knows how to invent things. Her inventions are on this paper."

Mackenzie took a closer look at the plastic figures. "What about Battle Ram?" he asked.

"Battle Ram can cook," said Katie. "He can dust."

Mackenzie pulled out a chair. "Mr. Dab can dust and cook," he said. "Battle Ram needs to work out. He needs a punching bag."

Katie didn't say anything. She was too busy drawing Yellow Melon's inventions.

Mackenzie got a rubber band and a balloon from the junk drawer. He got some rice from the tin on the counter. He sat at the table and started to make the punching bag.

The plastic doll with the spiky hair looked at him. She was holding a turquoise crayon. "That girl should do something too," Mackenzie said. "She can't just sit around all day."

"Her name is Destiny," said Katie. "She's going to clip the coupons from the newspaper."

Katie and Mackenzie stayed at the table for a long time.

Yellow Melon went to work at the office. She designed a pencil with a built-in computer. It never

made mistakes. She designed a lunch box with a magic meal-maker button.

Mr. Dab made banana shakes. Katie put chocolate sprinkles on her shake, and Mackenzie drank his shake with a strawberry straw.

Battle Ram made a booby trap to catch varmints. It had a falling trapdoor. He punched his punching bag.

Destiny cut out a coupon from the paper. She made a shopping list. Katie needed some clips for her hair. Mackenzie needed a haircut. Yellow Melon needed more paper.

Everybody had something to do. It was a very busy household.

"Hey," said Mackenzie. He pointed to the paper. One of the headlines said "Pothole Problems!"

Katie and Mackenzie stared at the paper. They stared at the picture of the pothole.

"That pothole has a problem all right," said Mackenzie. "That problem is George."

"Potholes belong in cheese," said Katie.

It was time for bed. Katie and Mackenzie put all the figures back on the shelf.

"Maybe George will turn up tomorrow," said Mackenzie.

"Maybe not," said Katie. "George has a mind of his own."

George
Goes to the Mall

George slid off the saddle. He felt all shook up. He looked around and around. In front of him was a giant shopping mall! It was lit up brighter than a birthday cake.

George grabbed the front seat of a shopping cart. There was a coupon for hair cement in the cart. It was just what he needed. A guy with flyaway parts could use some hair cement. Nobody wants to lose their hair!

A shiny coin fell into his lap. That was strange. Money doesn't grow on trees. You can't dig some up in your backyard. It's not supposed to fall from the sky. But this time it did.

Now he had a coin and a coupon.

He was George, the Rich Man!

There was no time to lose. George headed for the mall.

The Mall at Night

The mall was closed. Molly walked past the row of shopping carts. All the shoppers had gone home. She mopped the floor. She took all the junk out of the carts.

"Hey!" the cleaning lady said. "There's a coupon for hair cement in this cart." She put the coupon in her pocket.

She saw the little plastic figure and the loonie too. "Looks like I found myself a rich man," she said. She put the loonie in her pocket. The little plastic guy got to sit on top of her dustbin.

The mall speakers were playing a waltz. The music made Molly's toes twitch. "Why," she declared, "it's a shame to waste that song." She grabbed George's little

hands and danced him over the tiles. When the plastic guy put one foot forward, the other went too.

"You dance like you have two left feet," declared Molly. She sprayed the little plastic guy with her bottle of window wash and gave him a good wipe. Then she put him back on the dustbin.

A window repairman was fixing one of the mall windows. He saw the figure on Molly's dustbin. "Why, that's George!" he exclaimed. "My daughter Rosie drew a picture of that guy in her art class. I've got that drawing right here in my wallet."

He pulled out the drawing. He sure was proud of his daughter's picture. "That George gets around," he said.

Molly nodded. "He's a real Prince Charming, all right. He just needs some dance lessons."

The night watchman came by. He looked at George and frowned. "The mall is closed," he said. "Does that guy have a mall pass?"

"Sure," said the window repairman. He held out the picture of George.

"That's all right then," said the night watchman.

Molly put George back on the dustbin. At the fast-food court, she stuck him in a pot of flowers. "You hang out here," she said. "Somebody will buy you a donut for sure."

George stayed under the flowers for almost a week.

That didn't matter. He kept lots of other people busy anyway.

People Send Letters
to the Paper

Katie and Mackenzie were standing at the window when the paper arrived. They both grabbed a page.

Katie looked at the comics. "George is not here," she said.

Mackenzie looked at the car ads. "He's not here either," he said.

The rest of the paper was all over the table. They could see the Letters to the Editor page. The title said "George Gets Mail!"

"Wow!" said Mackenzie. "People are writing letters to George."

"Some people don't have enough to do," said Kate.

They read the letters.

Dear George,

You are way cool! I put your picture on my fridge. Now my dad is on a diet. He wants to look just like you.

Love ya,

Rosie

Dear George,

Stay out of my rose beds. And keep down the noise. I'm just an old man. I need my peace and quiet.

Yours truly,

Mr. Beasle

Dear George,

Greetings from the farm! Thank you for bringing me luck. Bob and I are going to marry. He's giving up his hobo ways.

Kindest regards,

Weetsie Lewis

Dear George,

Plastic is bad for the environment. You should be ashamed of yourself. You don't belong in the creeks. Creeks are for fish!

Sincerely,

J. Trout

Mon cher Georges,

Comment ça va? N'oublie pas de pratiquer tes verbes!

Amitié,

Mlle Lesage

"Maybe we should send a letter," said Mackenzie.

"Are you crazy?" Katie exclaimed. "George will get a swelled head."

"His head is pretty big already," said Mackenzie.

Katie took Yellow Melon, Battle Ram, Mr. Dab and Destiny down from the shelf.

Mackenzie gave Battle Ram his punching bag.

He made an apron out of a paper towel and put it over Mr. Dab's mackintosh. Katie drew a heart tattoo on Destiny's arm. She put a little ribbon with silver sparkles around the girl's dress. Yellow Melon drew a pair of magnetic mittens.

Katie put a first-prize ribbon on the mittens. Then she took a picture of the plastic people. Mackenzie e-mailed it to the editor of the *Scarborough Windows* newspaper.

When the editor got the picture, she smiled. "Look at these fans," she said. "George is a real scoop!"

Sho
Makes a Pet

Sho sat in his basement apartment. He read the story about the missing parts. He looked at the pothole picture. He read the letters to the editor.

"Everybody knows about George," he sighed.

Sho was an artist. He made figures out of wax. He could even shape tiny earlobes and knobby knees out of wax.

Sometimes a toymaker bought one of Sho's little wax guys for his toy factory. Then the factory would make lots of plastic guys that looked like the wax one.

When Sho sold a figure, he made enough money to buy hamburgers for a month. One month he got a plastic figure for free every time he bought a hamburger. Wasn't that strange? Sho sold one wax figure for thirty hamburgers and got thirty plastic figures for free.

Sho sighed again. "Too bad I didn't think of making that George."

Sho stared at the lump of wax in front of him. He needed to make another wax figure to sell. Soon he would need more hamburgers.

The paper arrived. Sho looked at the picture of Yellow Melon, Battle Ram, Mr. Dab and Destiny. Then he looked at the picture of George in the pothole. Hmmmm, he thought. They need a pet.

He began to sculpt a figure out of wax. He gave the pet a big belly and strong leg muscles. He gave it a mouth for smiling and snarling. He put some spiky hair behind the ears.

Finally the pet was finished. "I'll name it Belly Kong," Sho said to himself. "A pet like that should be worth a lot of hamburgers. It will fetch newspapers. It will eat leftover vegetables."

Sho needed a toymaker to buy Belly Kong. He went to get a piece of paper and a pencil.

Who knows why he did that?

Mrs. Beasle
Finds George

A few days later a little old lady went to the mall. It was early. She looked at the chrysanthemums in the food court. She bent down to smell the flowers.

Most people don't bother to smell the flowers in the food court. They like to smell the vinegar and the ketchup. They like to smell the onions. But Mrs. Beasle liked to smell the flowers.

When she bent down, she saw George. "Hello, young man," she said. "I'm just going to have a cup of tea. Would you like to join me?"

She picked up the little plastic guy. "Heavenly days!" she said. "You're sitting on a loonie. I guess it's you that's inviting me!"

Mrs. Beasle bought a tea. She sat down at the table. A girl washing tables stopped for a moment. "Morning, Mrs. Beasle," she said. "Is that your boyfriend?"

Mrs. Beasle blushed. "Why I'm sure Mr. Beasle would have something to say about that," she declared.

Mrs. Beasle shared her tea with George. Afterward she said, "You can help me shop. I might find a pair of shoes that fit."

She put George in her shopping basket. She put her purse in the basket too. Then she headed for the department store.

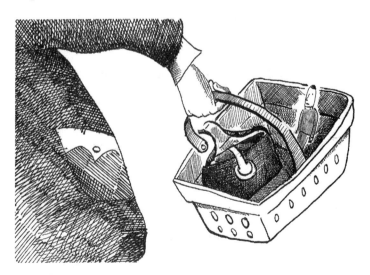

Katie and Mackenzie Look for George

Mackenzie and Katie walked to the mall with their mother.

They walked down the street past the pothole. Somebody had put big yellow lights beside the hole. The lights blinked on and off like an owl with a headache. Strips of yellow tape covered the hole.

"Look," Mackenzie said. "George's goggles are in that pothole. Battle Ram's helmet is there too."

"Excuse me," Kate said to a construction worker. "Could I have those plastic pieces?"

The construction worker handed Katie the goggles and the helmet. He winked at Mackenzie's mom.

They crossed the street and went into the mall.

"Wow!" said Mackenzie. "Johnny's Joy Town is set up in the parking lot. I'm going to go for a ride."

"I want to go on the Screamer," said Kate.

"I'm going on the Fun Slide," said Mackenzie.

The carnie was standing beside the white horse with the blue stars. "What about the merry-go-round?" he asked.

"Merry-go-rounds are for little kids," said Mackenzie.

After the ride the children asked the carnie, "Have you seen a guy in a red jumpsuit?"

"He was here," said the carnie. "He was headed for the mall last I saw."

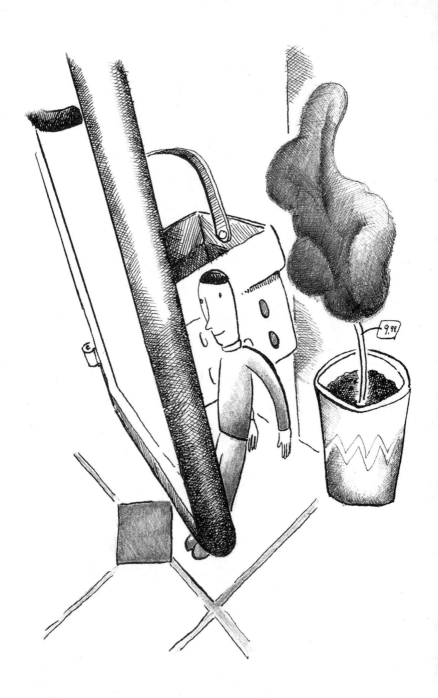

George
Stops a Thief

George woke up. He felt refreshed after his long sleep. He drank his breakfast tea and grabbed a basket. It was time to shop.

The department store was huge! George held his breath. Everything was super-sized. There were candles as big as traffic lights, hankies bigger than bedsheets, donuts as wide as truck tires.

He went to the garden department to look at the birdbaths. Suddenly someone banged into his cart.

Bump! Bumpety bump-bump!

The basket was running away. And he was in it!

George was not going to let a basket steal him. No way! He still had more shopping to do. He rolled over onto the floor and stuck his foot under the door. The other foot went too. Those two feet made the door jam.

The basket banged into the door one way. It slammed into the door another way. But the door didn't budge. And the basket was trapped in between. And so was the thief. George had stopped the thief!

Too bad one shiny red shoe was longer than the other. It had stretched. Now he had a thumb that was a little bit short. He had a foot that was a little bit long.

Who cares! Lots of people have parts that don't match. Some people even have parts that don't work.

He was George the Brave, George the Steadfast. Those things were way more important than a too-short thumb and a too-long foot!

Mr. Beasle
Is Sorry

"My purse! My purse!" cried the little old lady. "That thief tried to take my purse!" She pointed to the revolving door. A thief was stuck in the middle. She was as stuck as a penny in a piggy bank.

Everybody in the department store crowded around to see what was happening.

"I shouldn't have put my purse in the basket," said Mrs. Beasle.

A policeman pried up the bottom of the door and pulled out the little red shoe. It was a good thing the little red guy came too.

The police took the robber away. First she wanted to see George. "That guy is pretty gutsy," the robber said. "I didn't think anybody would catch me.

Nobody has ever caught me before." She got into the police car shaking her head.

The mall manager held up George so everybody could have a look at the thief nabber.

"Hurray for George!" somebody yelled. The crowd cheered.

All the people in the mall were surprised. A little plastic guy had stopped a robber. That guy had saved a lady's purse. The people went home and told their friends about George. Their friends told their friends. They told their relatives in Prince George. Folks even heard about him in Georgian Bay.

Someone in Paris read the story about George in an e-mail. Pretty soon the story went all the way around the world!

The *Scarborough Windows* newspaper put George on the front page. The headline said "George Foils Purse Snatcher." The paper quoted the thief.

"I'm sorry I tried to steal the lady's purse," said the thief. "That George taught me a lesson."

"Look at the paper," said Mrs. Beasle to her husband. She pointed to the headline. "That's the little guy that saved my purse. Our wedding picture was in that purse. That purse had our airline tickets to Florida."

The grumpy old man looked at the picture under the story. He looked at the little guy.

"Hmmm…" he said. "I think that guy lives next door."

"He's so brave," said his wife.

The grumpy old man felt bad. Why shouldn't he? He had tossed George's arm and hand over the fence. He had written a nasty letter to George and sent it to the paper.

Everybody knows that's no way to treat a neighbor.

The grumpy old man got out of his chair. He went to the shed and took out his garden shears.

The doorbell rang at Katie and Mackenzie's house. When they opened the door, they saw a rose on the porch. It was a big red rose. There was a note too.

Dear George,

Sorry old chap. You're a good neighbor. This is the last rose of the season. It's the best rose of all.

Regards,

Mr. Beasle

The Mall Has a George Day

The mall manager read the story about the foiled robbery attempt in the *Scarborough Windows*. There were more letters to George in the paper too. And there was a drawing from a fan. It was signed with a paw print.

The manager looked at the drawing carefully. He was impressed. "George has some pretty good fans," he said. "That Belly Kong looks like a good pet."

The articles about George gave the mall manager an idea. He had a meeting with all the store managers of the mall. They thought it was a good idea too. They put an ad in the *Scarborough Windows* newspaper. The ad said:

Mall Mania
Meet George in person!
Saturday October 2, 2:00
Free draw

The mall got ready for the big day. The department store ordered a hundred pairs of red shoes to sell. The hairdressing salon offered the George cut. The toy shop put a sign by their plastic figures that said *Buy Two, Get One Free.*

The donut store put a George donut on its shelves. It was called the Pothole Special.

All the stores put tables outside their stores. The tables were covered in red tablecloths. They were filled with things to buy for half price.

One table by the elevator had a big jam jar with an opening in the top. That jar was for the draw tickets. Anybody who bought something at the mall that day got a ticket for the draw.

A young man in a red jumpsuit and shiny red shoes stood next to the draw table. He gave away red helium balloons to people passing by.

That day the mall was as busy as the *a* in the word aardvark, busier than the *y* in a question. At two o'clock everybody went to the draw table.

All the shoppers wanted to talk about George.

The grumpy old man held his wife's hand. "Mrs. Beasle and I are George's neighbors," he said proudly. "George is a real nice chap."

"George came to see me when I had the measles," said a kid.

"We were dance partners," said Molly.

Even the carnie came by with Spy. "George likes to monkey around," said the carnie.

Katie and Mackenzie stood at the back of the crowd. "I put a ticket in the draw," said Mackenzie.

Katie didn't say anything. She was too busy looking at the guy with the red jumpsuit and the wavy black hair.

People started to chant. "We want George! We want George! We want George!"

The mall manager brought out George. He put George on the jam jar.

"George! George! George!" shouted the crowd. Some of the girls grabbed their faces and screamed. So did some of the boys. One boy cried.

Then it was time for the draw. The prize was an all-day pass at Johnny's Joy Town. Mr. Beasle won it. He gave it to Mr. Mohan's little boy.

Everybody went back to their shopping. The mall manager didn't know what to do with George.

When no one was looking, he put him on a table full of hair products.

Katie and Mackenzie Take George Home

Katie and Mackenzie walked by the tables in the mall.

George stood between a sample of hair cement and a package of curlers.

"Hey!" said Mackenzie. "There's George. I found George."

The saleslady at the table looked at them.

"That's George," said Katie to the saleslady. "He should go home with us."

The saleslady looked at the two kids. She looked at George. "He's sitting on a table with our hair products," she said. "There's a *For Sale* sign hanging over his head. You have to buy him."

"There's no price tag," said Mackenzie.

The saleslady looked at the toy.

"He's a customer," said Katie. "He wants to buy that hair cement."

The saleslady looked at the figure carefully. "He can't be a customer," she said. "He doesn't have any money."

"He has a coupon," said Katie. "Here it is." She held up the coupon. It was the one that Destiny had cut out of the paper.

"Oh," said the lady. "That's all right then!" She took the coupon and put the hair cement in a bag. "Er…," she said. "Would the customer like to go in the bag too?"

"I'll carry him," Katie said.

"Thank you for shopping at Mop Tops," the saleslady said. "Here's a balloon."

Katie carried George home. Mackenzie took care of the cement and the balloon.

The balloon bobbed on the wind. "Maybe George should go for a ride," said Mackenzie.

"Maybe tomorrow," said Kate. "Tonight he's invited for dinner."

A Toymaker
Buys Belly Kong

Sho got a phone call the day after the mall event. It was from a toymaker in Vancouver.

"I saw a drawing in the paper," the toymaker said. "How come I haven't seen Belly Kong before? My toy factory can make that pet. I want to buy that wax model."

The toymaker named a price.

Sho only had a few dollars left. He could only buy a few more hamburgers. But he kept his wits. "Belly Kong is worth more than that," he said. "It will be a faithful pet. Everyone will want to buy a figure like Belly Kong."

The owner of the factory hummed. He hawed. Finally he said a price that was a little bigger.

"Good-bye," said Sho. He pressed the end button on the telephone.

The phone rang again. Sho picked it up.

The toymaker named a new price. The price was a lot bigger.

"Bye," said Sho.

"Wait!" the toymaker cried. "How much do you want?"

Sho named the biggest price of all.

The toymaker gasped. Then he said okay.

That night Sho went to the hamburger shop. He took the girl behind the counter for a sushi platter downtown.

The Best of All

It was dark.

George sat beside his girl.

The girl was wearing a belt of silver stars. She twinkled at George.

George could hear the quick ticktock of a clock. He could hear the quiet drip of a tap. He could feel Destiny's hand in his hand.

Yellow Melon, Mr. Dab and Battle Ram sat there too. Yellow Melon was dreaming. Her eyes were closed. Maybe she was dreaming of another invention. Maybe it was a pillow plumper. Maybe it was a clutter spray.

Mr. Dab leaned against her. He was tired. He had made blackberry pancakes for dinner.

Battle Ram peered out from under his helmet. He would keep them safe all through the night.

There was a paper cutout on the shelf too. It was a strange pet with spiky hair. The paper pet leaned on Battle Ram's boots. Someone had colored it with a turquoise marker.

George sat quietly thinking. He looked at the giant hot-air balloon that floated in the air over his head. That balloon could wait for a bit.

He was George the Brave, George the Steadfast.

And he was most grateful.

He had friends.

He was a friend.

That was the best of all!

Ingrid Lee's unusual imagination is just as comfortable carrying her into the head of a small plastic toy, a dragon sand sculpture or an ordinary girl or boy. She lives in Toronto, Ontario. This is her third and final book about George.

Read all three books...
The True Story of George
George Most Wanted
George, the Best of All!